For Tony

VUTHY KUON

HUMPTY DUMPTY

After the Fall

Humpty Dumpty sat on a wall

Humpty Dumpty had a great fall.

All the king's horses and all the king's men

Couldn't put Humpty together again.

The doctor came, and told the nurse,

"We must check his heartbeat first!"

He then pulled out the stethoscope.

He listened, then he gave up hope.

"His heart don't beat, I think it's broke!"

Well, a heart can't beat if the heart's a yolk.

The nurse cried out in desperate fear,

Loud and clear, "Is the tailor here?"

The tailor came, did not fare well,

With every stitch he'd break the shell.

Humpty longed his same self be,

Back to one piece, not seventy.

The carpenter built him crutches of wood,

With rubber ends, but still weren't good.

Humpty said, "I can see your craft,

But what will I do with my other half?"

"Now who will help me?" Humpty cried,

"Three have failed, three have tried."

The welder came and willed to weld.

He scorched the shell and also failed.

"Don't burn the egg!" the baker said,

I will need the whites for bread.

"Then why don't you just take it all?"

"Nah... yolk is full of cholesterol."

Then the tax collector came,

The people ran, they feared his name.

"It's time to pay!" this he spoke.

Humpty said, " I can't... I'm broke!"

Left alone, the sun burned high

His yellow heart fried, as time went by.

But from above there came a dove

Whose open wings were arms of love.

And from his beak a loving voice,

Said, "Through your pain, you must rejoice!

Have faith, my friend, reach out your hand,

Now touch my wing, be one again."

He then stood up, his lesson learned.

He left his wall and ne'er returned.

Now his heart is full of bliss,

Humpty's story will go like this...

Humpty Dumpty after the fall,

Helped the needy at every call.

He vowed to the women and all the town's men

He'd never sit idle and be lazy again.